James Mayhew
presents

Ella Bella
BALLERINA
~ and ~
The Nutcracker

For Madison and Charlotte Davidson

with love J. M.

As always, my thanks to my editor Liz Johnson,
my designer Clare Mills and everyone at Orchard Books
for helping *Ella Bella* to keep on dancing!

ORCHARD BOOKS
338 Euston Road, London, NW1 3BH
Orchard Books Australia
Level 17/207 Kent Street, Sydney, NSW 2000

First published in 2012 by Orchard Books
First paperback publication in 2013

ISBN 978 1 40831 408 1

Text and illustrations © James Mayhew 2012

A CIP catalogue record for this book
is available from the British Library.

2 4 6 8 10 9 7 5 3 1

Printed in China

Orchard Books is a division of Hachette Children's Books,
an Hachette UK company.
www.hachette.co.uk

James Mayhew
presents

Ella Bella
✳ BALLERINA ✳
~ and ~
The Nutcracker

ORCHARD

Ella Bella's ballet class was about to begin.
Outside the old theatre it had started to snow
while, inside, the children were very excited.

"It's the perfect weather for today's lesson,"
smiled Madame Rosa, leading them to the stage.
There, a twinkling Christmas tree stood beside
Madame Rosa's special music box.

Madame Rosa opened the box and beautiful
music began to play.
"Let's dance to a waltz from *The Nutcracker* ballet,"
she said. "Can you all twirl like little snowflakes?"

"Is the ballet about snowflakes?" asked Ella Bella.
"Yes, and toys and fairies and even sweets, too,"
said Madame Rosa. "It all starts on Christmas Eve,
when magical things happen . . ."

"One Christmas, a girl called Clara is given a wooden
nutcracker by her Godfather," said Madame Rosa,
"but she doesn't know that the nutcracker is really
her Godfather's nephew!"
"How can that be?" asked Ella Bella.

"Well, the nutcracker is under a magic spell, cast by his arch enemy, the wicked Mouse King," explained Madame Rosa. "Now, I'd love to tell you more of the story but then we wouldn't have time for your surprise . . . follow me!"

She led the children to a room
where tables were covered
with sweets and treats.
"A party!" gasped the children.

"Ella Bella, would you fetch
the music box?" asked Madame
Rosa. "Then we can have some
dancing at our party!"

Ella Bella ran back to the stage. She couldn't resist opening the lid of the box, to listen to the magical music once more. All by herself, Ella danced and twirled and spun . . .

As she danced, Ella Bella suddenly noticed
a girl with a wooden nutcracker, sleeping under
the Christmas tree. The girl woke up and rubbed
her eyes.

"Hello, I'm Ella," said Ella Bella. "Do you want
to dance, too?"
"Oh, yes," said the girl. "My name's Clara and
I love dancing!"

They held hands and danced around the
Christmas tree. It seemed to grow taller and taller
until Ella Bella and Clara felt quite tiny beside it.

It was then they noticed lots of beady eyes
peering out of the darkness.
"We're surrounded by mice!" whispered Clara.
"How will we escape?"
Just then, the sound of trumpets filled the air!

The wooden nutcracker had come to life! He
marched forward with his toy soldiers to protect Ella
and Clara from the wicked Mouse King and his army.

"Oh, Nutcracker, do be careful!" called Clara.
The toy soldiers tried to scare the mice away
but they crept closer and closer . . .

"The Nutcracker needs our help," said Ella
Bella. "We should throw something at the
Mouse King!"

Clara took off a shoe and threw it as hard as she could at the Mouse King.
He fell to the ground, defeated. The other mice carried him away, and all was silent.

Clara and Ella Bella saw that the nutcracker
was no longer wooden; he was a handsome young
prince. The Mouse King's spell was broken!
"Thank you," he smiled, bowing. "I will reward
you by taking you to my magical kingdom!"

The Nutcracker Prince led
Clara and Ella Bella through
the branches of the Christmas
tree and into a snowy forest.
A magical sleigh carried
them up into the sky as
the snowflakes danced
all around them.

The sleigh flew through the snow to the Land of Sweets. "Welcome to my kingdom!" smiled the Nutcracker Prince. They stepped through gardens of sparkling sugar to the magnificent Marzipan Palace.

The Sugar Plum Fairy was
waiting to greet them.

The Sugar Plum Fairy clapped her hands and, as if by magic, chocolate from Spain, Arabian coffee and Chinese tea all danced for their guests. Soon all sorts of other sweets joined in.

"Isn't this the best Christmas party
ever?" asked Clara.

"Oh, yes! It's wonderful," laughed Ella Bella.

"Thank you again for saving me," said the Nutcracker.
"Perhaps one day you could be Queen in my kingdom."
"I'd like that," smiled Clara.
Then, the Sugar Plum Fairy performed her most
sparkling dance to show her gratitude.

Outside the palace, even the flowers were dancing.
Then, as the music grew fainter, the Marzipan
Palace seemed to fade, too.
Ella Bella took one last look around to be sure
she would always remember it.

The music stopped and Ella Bella
found herself beside the Christmas tree
once more. But Clara had gone.

Ella Bella heard the sounds of the party
and Madame Rosa peered onto the stage.
"Come and join us," she said.
"We've got marzipan fruits, sugar plums
and pink lemonade!"

"It looks like the Land of Sweets!" said Ella Bella.
"Yes, we even have mice!" smiled Madame Rosa.
"Real mice?" asked Ella Bella.
"Sugar mice!" laughed Madame Rosa.
"Let's see if there is one left . . . "

And, of course, there was!

The Nutcracker is one of the most loved of all ballets, and it's easy to see why, when it is filled with Christmas magic, twirling snowflakes and dancing sweets!

The original story was written in 1816 by a German writer called Ernst Hoffmann, and was called *The Nutcracker and the Mouse King*. It's a long and mysterious story about princesses and mice and magic. Only a small part of this extraordinary tale was used for the ballet.

The unforgettable music was written in 1892, by the Russian composer Piotr Tchaikovsky, for the magnificent Imperial Ballet at the Mariinsky Theatre in St Petersburg. Tchaikovsky was one of the first composers to use a new instrument called the celesta, which creates a delicate tinkling sound and is played during the most famous moment of all, *The Dance of the Sugar Plum Fairy*. But all the music glitters and sparkles with the sounds of snow and sugar!

In the performance, not only the dancers and musicians need to be wonderful, but the scenery has to be magical and astonishing, too. The

Christmas tree needs to grow taller and taller, and the Land of Sweets has to look delicious! Many ballet companies perform *The Nutcracker* every Christmas, to theatres full of enchanted children. After all, who can resist such a dazzling dancing delight?